The Boy With Green Thumbs and The Wild Tree Man

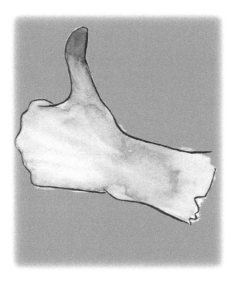

A short story by Larry W Jones

This is a work of fiction.

First edition - December 2020

Book design by Larry W Jones

Published by lulu.com

ISBN - 978-1-716-31763-7

Once upon a time there was a stately King who had strangely disappeared from his realm. There was a great green forest near his palace, full of all kinds of food growing therein upon the ground and on the trees.

One day the Prince, the King's son, sent out the chief gardener to gather green herbs for his dinner, but nay did the plantsman return. "Perchance some accident has befallen him," thought the Prince, and the next day he sent out two more gardeners to search for him, but nay did they return as well.

Then on the third day, he summoned all his gardeners, and said, "Scour the whole forest through, and do not give up until ye have found all three." But of these also, nay one of them returned to the palace of the Prince.

From that time whenceforth, the Prince forbade anyone to venture into the great green forest, and it lay in deep stillness and solitude. Nothing was seen in it except an occasional eagle or hawk flying above it.

This lasted for some years until an unknown gardener came to the Prince asking for work, and offered to go into the dangerous forest to gather herbs. The Prince, however, was reluctant to give his consent, and said, "It is not safe in there. I fear it would fare with you no better than with the others, and you would never come out again."

The gardener replied, "My Lord and Prince, I will venture in at my own risk. I know nothing of fear." The gardener therefore proceeded with his pet hound to the forest. It was not long before the hound saw a wild hare and pursued it to a hole beneath a giant oak tree and could go no farther.

Suddenly, a knobby arm stretched itself out from the tree, seized the hound, and drew it underneath the bark.

When the gardener saw that, he went back and fetched more men to come with axes and cut down the tree. When they got to the tree, there they saw a Wild Tree Man whose body was green and mossy like wet bark, and whose hair hung down to the ground.

Instead of cutting the tree down, they dug it up by the roots and carried it away to the castle.

There was great astonishment over the Wild Tree Man. The Prince had him put in a tall iron cage in his courtyard, and forbade the door to be opened on pain of death, and his mother, the Queen herself, was to take the key into her keeping.

Now, from this time forth, with the Wild Tree Man in custody, anyone could once more go into the forest with safety.

Now, the King who disappeared had a servant boy, who one day was playing in the courtyard. While he was playing, his golden ball fell into the cage. The boy ran thither and said to the Wild Tree Man, "Give me my ball." "Not until you have unlocked the cage door for me," answered the Wild Tree Man.

"No," said the boy, "I will not do that. My master, the missing King and his son, the Prince, both have forbidden it," and the boy ran away. The next day he again went and asked for his ball. The Wild Tree Man said, "Open my cage door." But the boy would not.

On the third day when the Prince had ridden out hunting, the boy went once more and said, "I cannot open the cage door even if I wished, for I have not the key." Then the Wild Tree Man said, "It lies under the Queen's pillow. You can get it there."

The boy, who wanted to have his ball back, cast all fear to the winds, and brought the key. The tall iron door was opened with difficulty, and the boy pinched his fingers. When it was open, the Wild Tree Man stepped out on his roots, gave the boy his golden ball, and hurried away as fast as his roots could run. But the boy was afraid. He called and cried after him, "Oh, Wild Tree Man, do not go away, or I shall be beaten by the Prince!" The Wild Tree Man turned back, took him up, set him upon one of his limbs and went with hasty steps back into the forest.

When the Prince came home, he saw the empty tall iron cage, and asked his mother, the Queen, how that had happened. She knew nothing about it, and sought the key, but it was gone. She called the servant boy, but no one answered. The Prince sent out people to seek for him in the palace gardens but they did not find him. Then the Prince could easily guess what had happened. The boy had been taken into the forest by the Wild Tree Man. Much grief reigned in the Royal Court.

When the Wild Tree Man had reached the great green forest, he took the boy down from his limb and said to him, "You may never see the Prince and Queen again, but I will keep you with me, for you may be able to set me free somehow. If you do all I bid you, you shall fare well. I was once the King but was turned into this Wild Tree Man. Of treasure and gold have I plenty, hidden in a secret well here in the forest." He made a bed of moss for the boy on which to sleep.

The next morning, the Wild Tree Man took him to his secret well, and said, "Behold, the well is full of gold and as bright and clear as crystal. You shall sit beside it, and take care that nothing falls into it, or it will be polluted. I will come every evening to see if you have obeyed my order."

The boy placed himself by the wall of the well, and often saw a golden fish or a golden snake show itself therein, and he took care that nothing fell in. But as he was sitting thus, his left thumb began to hurt him so violently that, without thinking, he dipped it in the water. He drew it quickly out again, but saw that his thumb was quite gilded like a shiny green emerald. And whatsoever effort he took to wash the emerald coloring off, all was to no purpose.

In the evening, the Wild Tree Man came back, looked at the boy, and said, "What has happened to the well?"

"Nothing, nothing," he answered, and held his left thumb behind his back so the Wild Tree Man might not see it. But he said to the boy, "You have dipped your thumb into the water and your thumb has turned green. This time I will let it pass, but take care you do not again let anything get in the well." At daybreak the boy was already sitting by the well and watching it. This time his right thumb began to hurt him exceedingly and he dipped it into the water as he had done with his left thumb. When he took it quickly out, it was quite gilded in color like a shiny green emerald.

When the Wild Tree Man came, he already knew what had happened. "You have dipped your other thumb into the well, turning your thumb green" said he. "I will allow you to watch by the well once more, but if this happens the third time, then the well will be polluted, and you can no longer remain with me."

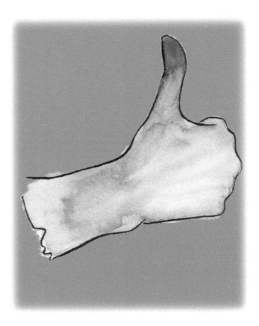

On the third day, the boy sat by the well, and did not dare stir his fingers however much his thumbs hurt him. But the time spent guarding the well was long to him, and he looked at the reflection of his face on the surface of the water. As he bent down more and more, trying to look straight into the eyes of his image, his long hair fell down from his shoulders and touched the water. He raised himself up quickly, but the whole of the hair of his head was now emerald green and shone as if the sun had green rays.

You may imagine how terrified the poor boy was! He took his bandana scarf and tied it around his head, in order that the Wild Tree Man might not see his green hair.

When the Wild Tree Man came, he already knew everything, and said, "Take off the bandana scarf." Then the boy's emerald green hair streamed forth. Let the boy excuse himself as he might, it was of no use. "You have not stood the trial, and can no longer stay here. Go forth into the world outside this great green forest. Here you had plenty to eat. Out there you will learn what poverty is. But, as you have not a bad heart, and as I mean well by you because you are a good boy, there is one thing I will grant you. If you fall into any difficulty, come to the forest and cry out, 'Wild Tree Man' and then I will come and help you. My kingly power is still great, greater than you think, and I have gold and silver in abundance."

Then the boy with the green thumbs left the forest, and walked by beaten and unbeaten paths ever onward, until at length he reached the palace of the Prince.

Wearing gloves to hide his green thumbs and an oversized hat to hide his emerald green hair, he looked for work, but could find none, and he had learnt nothing by which he could help himself.

At length, he went to the Prince and asked if they would take him in. The people at the Court did not know what use to make of him, but they liked him because of his politeness, and told him to stay. At last, the royal cook took him into his service, and said that he might wash the pots, pans and dishes and serve food to the Queen, to her son the Prince, and to the Prince's beautiful young sister.

Once when it happened that no one else was at hand, the cook ordered him to carry the food to the royal table, but as he did not like to let his emerald green hair be seen, he kept his oversized hat on. Such a thing as that had never come under the Queen's or the Prince's notice, and the Queen said, "When you serve at the royal table you must take off your hat."

The boy with the gloved green thumbs answered, "Ah, my Lady the Queen, I cannot." Then the Prince had the cook called before him. He scolded him, and asked how he could take such a boy as that into his service and said that he was to release him from royal service at once. The cook, however, had pity on him, and exchanged him for the chief gardener's boy.

And soon, the servant boy with the green thumbs had grown up into a fine young man and continued to plant and water the garden, hoe and dig, and bear the wind and bad weather. One day in summer when he was working alone in the garden, the day was so warm he took his oversized hat off so that the air might cool him.

As the sun shone on his emerald green hair it glittered and flashed so that the rays reflected off the window into the bedroom of the missing King's daughter, the sister of the Prince.

Up she sprang to see what it could be. Then she saw the young man with the green thumbs and green hair, and cried out to him, "Young man, bring me a bouquet of field-flowers."

He put his hat on with all haste, and gathered wild field-flowers and bound them together. When he was ascending the stairs with them, the chief gardener met him, and said, "How can you take the King's daughter a garland of such common flowers? Go quickly, and get another, and seek out the prettiest and rarest." "Oh no," replied the boy, "the wild ones have more sweet scent, and will please her all the more."

When he went into the room, the King's daughter said, "Take your hat off. It is not seemly to keep it on in my presence." He again said, "I cannot." She, however, grabbed his hat and pulled it off, and then his emerald green hair rolled down on his shoulders. And to her it was splendid and pleasing to behold.

He wanted to run out, but she held him by the arm, and gave him a handful of golden ducats. With these he departed, but he cared nothing for the gold pieces. He took them to the chief

gardener, and said, "I give them to you for your children so that they may play with them."

The following day, the King's daughter again called to him that he was to bring her a bouquet of field-flowers. When he went in with it, she grabbed at his hat and wanted to take it away from him, but he held it fast with both gloved hands. She again gave him a handful of golden ducats. But he would not keep them, and presented them to the chief gardener as playthings for the gardener's children. On the third day, things went just the same. But she could not get his hat away from him, and he would not take her golden ducats.

Not long afterward, the Prince's dominion was overrun by a great famine. The Prince gathered together his people and told them that he did not know whether or not his missing father's kingdom could survive the famine which was causing starvation among the people. He begged if there was anyone who might come forward with ideas.

Then spoke up the chief gardener's young man, "I am now grown up, and will go to the fields to plow and cultivate. Only give me an oxen." The people laughed, and said, "Seek an oxen for yourself. There is one in the King's

stable." The young man with the green thumbs went into the stable, and got the oxen. But it was lame on one foot, and limped on three legs. "This oxen is useless for plowing a field." the young man said. Nevertheless he carefully harnessed it, and gently led it away to the great green forest.

When he came to the outskirts of the forest, he called "Wild Tree Man" three times so loudly that his voice echoed through the forest. Thereupon the Wild Tree Man appeared and said, "What do you desire?" "I want a strong oxen, for I am going to plow the fields and plant greens for food to end the famine." "That you shall have, and still more than you ask." Then the Wild Tree Man went back into the forest. It was not long before a stable-boy came out of it, who led two big green oxen that snorted, and could hardly be restrained because of their power. The Wild Tree Man said "These two big green oxen can plow a thousand acres a day and never tire out."

Behind the oxen followed a great crowd of gardeners equipped with plows, shovels, rakes and all manner of cultivating tools. The young man with the green thumbs gave over his lame oxen to the stable-boy, took hold of the two big green oxen, and walked at the head of the army of gardeners. When he drew near the fields of famine, a great many of the Prince's people had already fallen in death from starvation, and few were wanting to even try to plant and grow food anymore.

Then the young man with the green thumbs walked thither with his green oxen and army of gardeners. They plowed, planted and cultivated like a tempest over the fields, and the fields produced food in abundance for all the people of the kingdom. They reaped the fields of so much food that the wagons could barely hold the heavy loads on the way back to the palace.

While returning to the Prince, the young man conducted his army of gardeners by a side-road back to the great green forest and called out for the Wild Tree Man. "What do you desire?" asked the Wild Tree Man. "Take back your two green oxen and army of gardeners, and give me the King's lame oxen again." All that he asked was done, and soon he was leading the King's lame oxen toward the palace stables.

When the Prince returned to his palace, his sister went to meet him, and wished the Prince joy for his hunting victory. The Prince told his sister, "A funny thing happened. While I was hunting in the forest, a strange young man with green thumbs came marching out of the forest with an army of gardeners."

The Prince's sister wanted to hear who the strange young man was, but the Prince did not know, and said, "He went out of the forest and into the fields with his army of gardeners who were carrying all sorts of cultivating tools. After that, I did not see him again."

She inquired of the Prince's chief gardener where his young man was, but the gardener smiled, and said, "He has just come home with the King's lame oxen and the people have been mocking him, and crying out, 'Here comes our lame oxen back again!' They also asked of him, 'Upon what field have you been lying sleeping all this time?' He, however, answered them, 'I did the best I could, and the fields would have produced badly without me." The people scoffed and asked, "What fields have produced anything?" and then he was ridiculed still more." Then the long procession of wagons loaded down with produce arrived at the palace. All were in amazement and quit their ridiculing of the young man, for the famine was over and the kingdom was saved from starvation.

The Prince said to his sister, "I will proclaim a great fun faire and feast that shall last for three days, and you shall throw to the knights a golden apple which looks beautiful but cannot be eaten, for nobody can survive on what is not real food. Perhaps some unknown happening will come of it."

When the fun faire and feast was announced, the young man went out to the great green forest, and called for the Wild Tree Man. "What do you desire?" asked he. "That I may catch the Prince's sister's golden apple when thrown at the festival." "It is as safe as if you had caught it already," said the Wild Tree Man. "You shall likewise have a knight's suit of emerald armor for the occasion, and ride on a spirited emerald colored horse."

When the day of the feast came, the young man galloped to the spot, took his place amongst the royal knights, but was recognized by no one.

The Prince's sister came forward, and threw a golden apple toward the knights. None of them caught it but he, and as soon as he had it, the apple turned a beautiful and delicious green, ready to eat. Then he galloped away.

On the second day, the Wild Tree Man equipped him as a white knight, and gave him a white horse. Again he was the only one who caught the apple, and as soon as he had it, the apple turned a beautiful and delicious green, ready to eat. Then he galloped off with it.

The Prince grew angry, and said, "That is not allowed. He must appear before me and tell me his name." He gave the order that if the knight who caught the apple should go away again, the other knights should pursue him, and, if he would not come back willingly, they should cause his demise in the forest.

On the third day, he received from the Wild Tree Man a knight's suit of black armor and a black horse.

Again he caught the golden apple, and as soon as he had it, the apple turned a beautiful and delicious green, ready to eat. But when he was riding off with it, the Prince's knights pursued him, and one of them got so near behind him that he wounded the young man's leg with the point of his sword. The young man nevertheless escaped from them, but his horse leapt so violently that the helmet fell from his head, and they could see that he had emerald green hair. They rode back and announced this to the Prince.

The following day, the King's daughter asked the chief gardener about the whereabouts of his apprentice. "He is at work in the garden. The young man has been at the festival too, and only came home yesterday evening. He has likewise given to my children three emerald green apples, good to eat, which he had won." The King's daughter was in wonder because she knew the apples she had thrown to the knights were all golden.

The Prince had the gardener's apprentice summoned into his presence. He came and again had his oversized hat on his head. But the Prince's sister went up to him and took it off. Then his emerald green hair fell down over his shoulders, and he was so handsome that all were amazed. The King's daughter knew immediately who he was.

"Are you the knight who came every day to the festival, always in different colors, and who caught the three golden apples?" asked the Prince. "Yes," answered he, "but the apples turned from useless gold to beautiful and delicious green apples, good for food." "You say the golden apples turned into green apples, good for eating?" asked the Prince. "Yes," said the young man. "Everything I touch seems to turn into good food for eating." "I am the knight who caught the golden apples and rode away. If you desire further proof, you may see the wound on my leg which your one of your knights gave me when they followed me into the great green forest. But I am likewise the one who helped your kingdom win victory over the great famine which was causing starvation among your people."

"If you can perform such deeds as that, you are no common gardener's boy. Tell me, who is your benefactor?" "My benefactor said he was once a mighty King, and gold in plenty he still has, hidden in a secret well in the forest. But he was turned into a Wild Tree Man." "I well see," said the Prince, "that I owe thanks to you. Can I do anything to please you?" "Yes," answered he, "Tell me how to return the Wild Tree Man to his human form and be the King he used to be." "Also, give me the hand of the King's daughter, your sister, as wife."

The Prince laughed, and said, "You do not stand much on ceremony, but I have already seen by your emerald green hair that you are no mere gardener's boy. Here, throw this golden apple to the Wild Tree Man. It has done marvelous things, so, who knows what it's effect will be? Perhaps the Wild Tree Man will become human again and will regain his throne." Then the King's daughter went and kissed the young man and a great wedding was planned at the palace.

As the wedding plans were being made, the young man with the green thumbs went to the edge of the forest and called out for the Wild Tree Man. "What do you wish this time?" asked the Wild Tree Man. "Here, catch this golden apple!" as he threw it toward the forest. The Wild Tree Man reached out a limb and caught the golden apple.

As soon as he had it, a handsome, royal figure in King's clothing stepped out from under the bark of the tree. It was the long missing King himself in all his majesty!

Beside him, wagging his tail, was the gardener's pet hound.

 The King threw the golden apple back to the young man but he missed catching it and it hit him on the head. Bonk! As soon as he removed his oversized hat, his hair fell down around his shoulders in a beautiful yellow-gold color.

The young man's father and mother came to the wedding, and were in great delight, for they had given up all hope of ever seeing their dear son again.

As they were sitting at the marriage feast, the music suddenly stopped, the palace doors opened, and a stately King came in with great fanfare. The Queen, the Prince, and his sister were astonished and joyful beyond words to have the King back in his palace.

The King went up to the young man with the green thumbs and yellow-gold hair, embraced him and said, "I am the rightful King, who was by enchantment turned into the Wild Tree Man. But you have set me free from the great green forest and saved my kingdom from famine.

I knew you as a good boy and now a fine young man fit for my daughter in marriage. You do not care for wealth or high position. You turned down gold ducats and gave them to my royal gardener's children and you acted kindly with my lame oxen.

By royal decree, I hereby proclaim that you and your new bride, my daughter, along with your parents, will sit at my dining table with me, my Queen, and my son the Prince, for as long as ye may live.

Behold, all ye merry men and women of the realm! This account shall be written into the royal archives as a remembrance of the fine deeds of the boy with green thumbs."

About the Author

Larry W Jones is a songwriter, having penned over 7,700 song lyrics. Published in 22 volumes of island themed, country, cowboy, western and bluegrass songs. The entire assemblage is the world's largest collection of lyrics written by an individual songwriter.

As a wrangler on the "Great American Horse Drive", at age 68, he assisted in driving 800 half-wild horses 62 miles in two days, from Winter pasture grounds in far NW Colorado to the Big Gulch Ranch outside of Craig Colorado.

His book, "The Oldest Greenhorn", chronicles the adventures and perils in earning the "Gate-to-Gate" trophy belt buckle the hard way.

This book, "The Boy With Green Thumbs and The Wild Tree Man" is his third short-story. The other two are "A Squirrel Named Julie and The Fox Ridge Fox" and "Up and Over – A Hike In The Rockies"
All his publications are available on Lulu.com.

CPSIA information can be obtained
at www.ICGtesting.com
Printed in the USA
BVHW020155291220
596493BV00004BA/7